For Oliver, William and Lara

An Imprint of Sterling Publishing
387 Park Avenue South
New York, NY 10016

SANDY CREEK and the distinctive Sandy Creek logo
are registered trade marks of Barnes & Noble, Inc.

First published in 2013 in Great Britain by Orchard Books,
an imprint of Hachette Children's Books.

Text and illustrations © John Butler 2013

This 2013 edition published by Sandy Creek.

Design by Ali Ardington

ISBN 978-1-4351-4769-0

Manufactured in China

Lot #:
2 4 6 8 10 9 7 5 3

08/14

# If Your Dreams Take Off And Fly

## John Butler

Sandy Creek
NEW YORK

When the night is very dark
And the moon is shining high,
Let your dreams take to the skies
Like a dancing butterfly.

You will travel to a place
Where koalas you will see,
And kangaroos and platypuses
Running wild and free.

Then you'll leave them all behind
As you flutter to the sky,
Looking for adventure,
My little butterfly.

Out across the oceans,
Watching whales as you pass by,
With all the world beneath you,
Your dreams go flying high.

Then floating over icebergs,
Where the icy, cold winds blow,
You'll see penguins as they huddle,
Finding shelter in the snow.

And when you reach the desert,
Where warm winds blow the sand,

There'll be a baby camel
Trotting out across the land.

Over grasslands and full rivers
You'll be floating in your dream,
While a family of hippos
Will be playing by a stream.

Drifting over forests,
As swallows swoop so fast,

A squirrel and a dormouse
Will watch as you glide past.

Then, flitting one last time
In the yellow setting sun,

You'll hear the sound of songbirds
As their lullaby is sung.

You will see so many things
And you will realize why,
Like you, this world is precious,
My little butterfly.

Our world is full of wonder
And your journey's just begun.
All you see around you
Is there for everyone.

And now it's time to sleep,
But remember, if you try,
Anything can happen
If your dreams take off and fly.